ISBN 0 86112 984 9
© Brimax Books 1995. All rights reserved.
Published by Brimax Books, Newmarket, England CB8 7AU 1995.
Printed in Dubai.

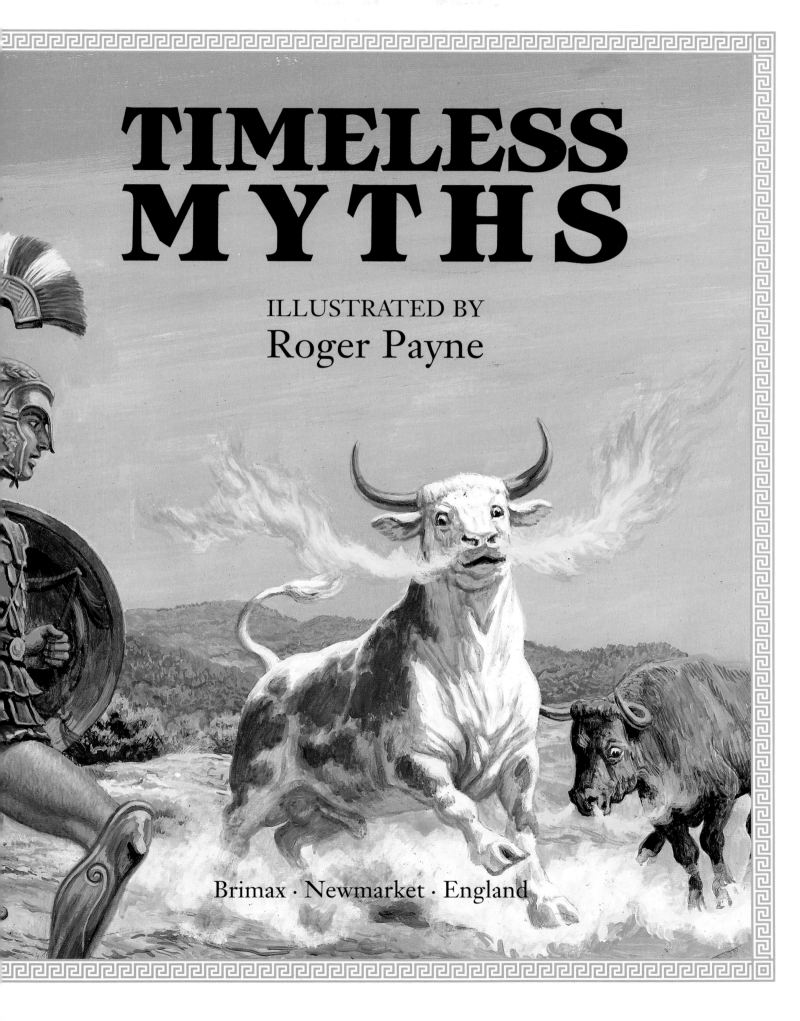

TIMELESS
MYTHS

ILLUSTRATED BY
Roger Payne

Brimax · Newmarket · England

Introduction

This collection of mythical adventures has fascinated people for thousands of years. No one will ever know if the terrible Minotaur ever existed or if there really was a winged horse called Pegasus.

But behind all these fantastic stories there lies some truth. Perhaps the people within these stories really did exist, but over many years the stories surrounding them have become more and more outrageous until the true facts have all but disappeared. Whether true or not, Timeless Myths retells magical tales of fantastic feats and events that will captivate all who read them.

Contents

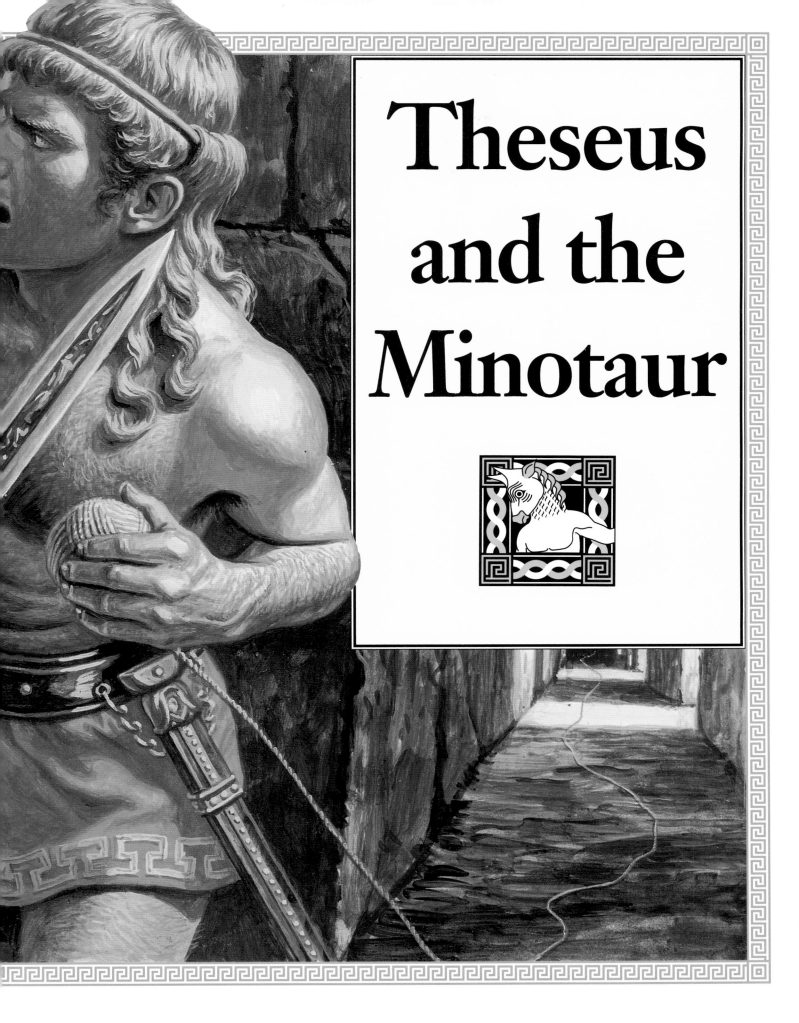

Theseus
and the
Minotaur

It was very dark inside the tunnel. Only a little moonlight came in through the holes in the roof. It was cold, too. Theseus shivered.

Already, he could hear the monster, Minotaur, roaring and stamping inside the labyrinth. It sounded hungry and angry. But there were so many tunnels in the labyrinth that Theseus could not tell where the sound was coming from. He would have to go deeper into the labyrinth if he was going to find the monster and kill it.

Deeper into the labyrinth! What a frightening thought! No one who had entered the labyrinth had ever found the way out again. All had been killed and eaten by the Minotaur.

Theseus' fingers closed tightly over the ball of thread in his hand. His other hand gripped hard on the hilt of his sword. A sword, a ball of thread and, in the pocket of his tunic, a small golden phial. That was all he had to fight against the mighty Minotaur. The Minotaur was a bloodthirsty creature. It had the body of a man, but the head and the strength of a bull and fangs as sharp as a lion's.

No wonder Theseus' father, King Aegeus of Athens, had wept when he learned that his son was going to Crete to try to kill the Minotaur.

"I shall never see you again, Theseus," the King had said, tears streaming down his face. "Must you go? I am an old man. I need you here, to help me govern my kingdom."

Theseus was very sad to see his father so upset, but he could not do as he wanted.

"If I don't kill this monster," Theseus told Aegeus, "you will have to send more and more young Athenians to provide it with food every year. Just think how many have already died!"

King Aegeus sighed deeply. Theseus was right. The young people of Athens had paid a dreadful price. Years ago, King Minos' son had been killed in Athens. In revenge, Minos demanded that fourteen Athenians – seven young men and seven girls – should be sent to Crete. There they were fed to the terrible Minotaur. If this was not done, then Minos threatened to attack and destroy Athens with his powerful army. However, if the young Athenians managed to kill the Minotaur, then Minos promised to stop demanding the yearly sacrifice.

'Oh, King Minos is cunning and cruel,' thought King Aegeus. 'He makes it impossible for anyone to kill the Minotaur by forbidding them to take weapons with them into the labyrinth.'

From the window of his palace, Aegeus could see the great ship with the black sail which made the sad journey to Crete every year. Aegeus saw fathers like himself weeping with terrible grief as they watched their sons and daughters climbing into the ship. Sadly Aegeus knew that Theseus must go with them.

"See how my people suffer!" sighed Aegeus. "If their children have to face the Minotaur, it is not right for their King to keep his own son safely at home."

Aegeus turned away from the window and said to Theseus, "We must say farewell, my son. I shall pray to all the gods on Olympus to protect you."

Aegeus picked up a small, golden phial that lay on the table nearby and gave it to Theseus. "This is from your stepmother, Medea. She says it will help you fight the Minotaur. As for me, I have one request to make of you."

"What is it, Father?" Theseus asked.

Aegeus gave him a large red square of material. "If you return safely from Crete, hoist this red sail from your ship when you come within sight of our shores."

Theseus smiled at his father, hoping to comfort him with cheerful words.

"My ship will have no black sail, Father," he told Aegeus. "This red sail will be flying from its mast when I return."

The voyage to Crete was a very sorrowful one. The fourteen Athenians could think only of the Minotaur and the terrible fate which awaited them. They wept and trembled. They grew more and more terrified as the ship approached its destination.

Theseus, however, was determined to show King Minos a brave face when he confronted him at his palace.

"What is the Prince of Athens doing here?" Minos demanded, recognising Theseus at once. "Surely King Aegeus has not sent his son to be sacrificed to the Minotaur?"

Theseus looked at Minos defiantly. "I have not come to be eaten by the monster," he answered. "I have come to kill it. Only then will my people be free from your terrible revenge."

At this, there was a great buzz of talk among the courtiers and nobles who surrounded Minos.

The King smiled a cruel smile. "Brave words, young Theseus," he said. "But the Minotaur is not so easy to kill when you have no weapons."

"I shall find a way to kill it," Theseus replied in a firm voice.

Princess Ariadne, King Minos' daughter, had been watching Theseus closely. Theseus was young, brave and strong, that was easy to see. Even so, he would need help if he were to succeed.

Ariadne made up her mind there and then that she would help Theseus in this difficult and dangerous task.

That night, Ariadne stayed awake for many hours until she was sure her father and his courtiers were asleep. Then she picked up a large vessel of wine and a ball of thread and crept from her room. Quickly and quietly, Ariadne passed along the corridors which led to the rooms where Theseus and his companions were staying. The sentries ouside the doors were surprised to see

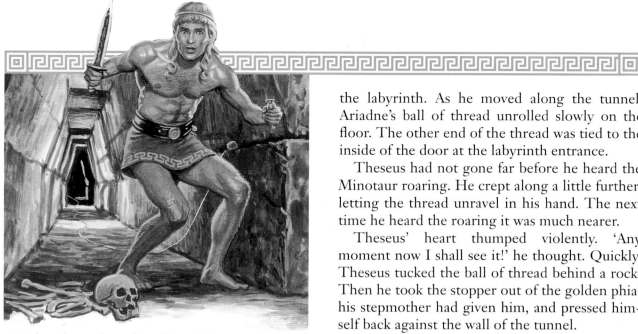

Ariadne, but when she offered them some wine, they were pleased.

"The night is long and there are cold winds blowing here," Ariadne said, smiling graciously. "Some wine will warm you."

The sleeping drug which Ariadne had put in the wine took a little while to work. A few minutes later, all the sentries were lying on the floor fast asleep.

Ariadne knocked quickly on the door of Theseus' room. He was surprised to see her and amazed when he heard what she had to say.

"I have come to help you, Theseus," Ariadne whispered. "Here, take this ball of thread, and a sword from one of the sentries."

"But why are you doing this?" Theseus asked in surprise. "Are you not afraid to anger your father?"

"My father is a cruel man," sighed Ariadne. "He feels no pity for those who die in the labyrinth! The only way to stop his cruelty is to kill the Minotaur … but we must not waste time! We must get to the labyrinth as quickly as possible."

Quietly, Theseus took a sword from one of the sleeping sentries and followed Ariadne out into the palace gardens and across the courtyard to the labyrinth. By the time they reached the entrance, Ariadne had told Theseus all he had to do.

A few minutes later, Theseus was inside the labyrinth. As he moved along the tunnel, Ariadne's ball of thread unrolled slowly on the floor. The other end of the thread was tied to the inside of the door at the labyrinth entrance.

Theseus had not gone far before he heard the Minotaur roaring. He crept along a little further, letting the thread unravel in his hand. The next time he heard the roaring it was much nearer.

Theseus' heart thumped violently. 'Any moment now I shall see it!' he thought. Quickly, Theseus tucked the ball of thread behind a rock. Then he took the stopper out of the golden phial his stepmother had given him, and pressed himself back against the wall of the tunnel.

Suddenly the Minotaur was before him. It was roaring, stamping and shaking its great, thick fists at the roof of the labyrinth which imprisoned it.

"Ugh! It's horrible!" Theseus murmured in disgust. In the dim light, Theseus saw the Minotaur's wide shoulders, the sharp horns in its bull's head and its wild, glaring eyes.

The eyes were glaring straight at Theseus. With a tremendous howl, the Minotaur leapt at him. But before the monster could seize him, Theseus threw the powder from the phial directly into its face. The Minotaur bellowed as the powder filled its eyes and mouth. It staggered back, coughing. It pounded its eyes with its fists. For that moment, the Minotaur was helpless.

Theseus sprang forward. He swung his sword and slashed at the monster's legs. The Minotaur crashed to the floor, roaring in pain. It clutched wildly at the walls of the tunnel, trying to push itself on to its feet again. All the while, its jaws were snapping at the attacker it could not see.

Theseus stayed back and waited until the Minotaur had exhausted itself. At last the monster lay gasping and panting on the floor. Its arms flopped motionless beside its hairy body.

Again Theseus leapt forward. He held his sword above his head. With all his strength he plunged the sword down and buried it in the Minotaur's heart. The Minotaur shrieked. Then the wild glare in its eyes faded. It was dead.

"The great gods be thanked!" cried Theseus, as he knelt beside the body of the monster. Suddenly Theseus felt pity for it. "It was not its fault it was born half-man, half-bull," he said. "Perhaps it is better for it to be dead than to live imprisoned in the labyrinth."

It was time to leave and join Ariadne, who was waiting outside. Theseus picked up the ball of thread from behind the rock where he had placed it. He walked back along the tunnel following the line of thread lying on the floor. Gradually, Theseus wound up the thread until at last he reached the entrance of the labyrinth.

When Theseus stepped out into the fresh, cool air of the night, Ariadne nearly cried with joy to see him.

"We must get away from Crete as fast as we can," Theseus told her. "You must come with us, Ariadne. If it became known how you helped us, you would be in great danger."

Ariadne nodded in agreement.

Swiftly, Theseus and Ariadne ran back into the palace, where the drugged sentries were sleeping. They roused the fourteen young Athenians and together they crept down to the harbour. When they ran on board the ship, the captain was amazed to see them.

"Get out to sea at once!" Theseus ordered. "Hurry! Hurry!"

It was still dark when the ship sailed out to sea and headed back to Athens but it was a joyful voyage, quite unlike the one that had brought the ship to Crete.

A few days later, Athens' harbour came into sight. In the excitement of his victory over the Minotaur, Theseus forgot his promise to his father. When King Aegeus saw the ship flying the black sail, he thought Theseus was dead.

"I cannot bear to live any longer," he cried.

King Aegeus threw himself into the sea and was never seen again.

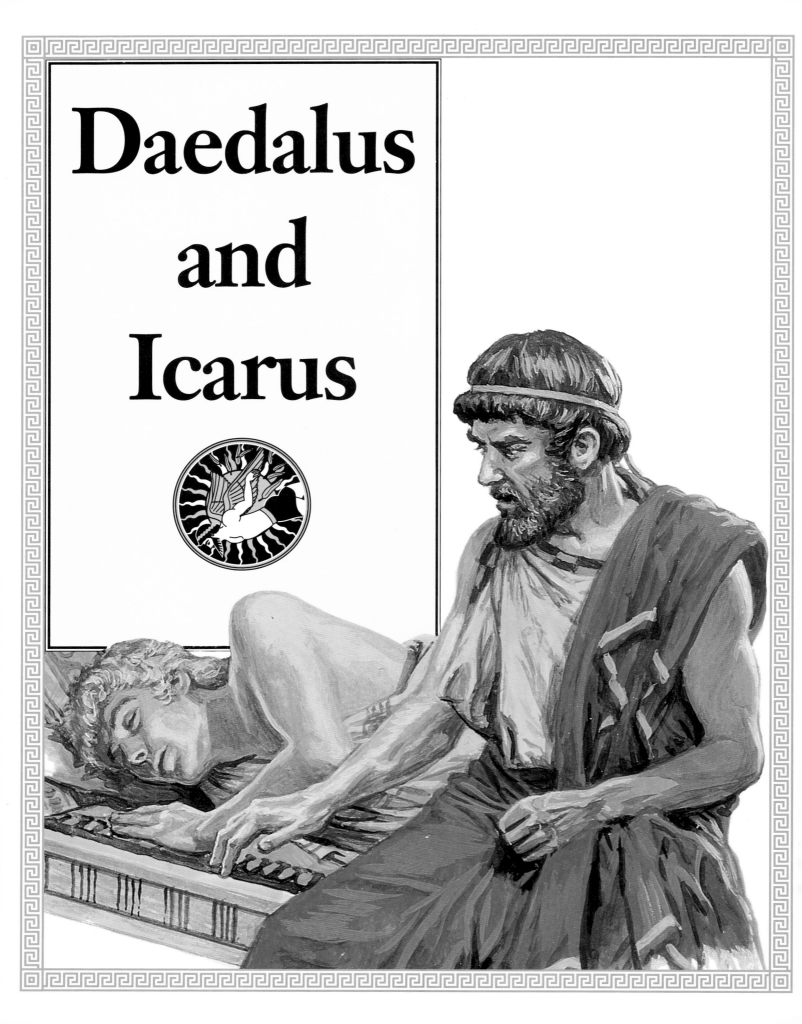

Daedalus
and
Icarus

"**I**carus! Wake up! Wake up!" Daedalus was sorry that he had to shake his son so roughly, but it was important that he woke up quickly. He and his father were in great danger. Any moment now, King Minos' guards would be outside the door. Daedalus shook his son again.

"Come on, Icarus!" he cried. "Wake up! By all the gods, why does the boy have to sleep so soundly?" Daedalus muttered. But then, everyone in the palace of Minos had been sound asleep the previous night when cunning Prince Theseus of Athens entered the labyrinth and killed the Minotaur imprisoned there. Everyone was fast asleep when Theseus sailed with the fourteen young Athenians who had come with him to the island of Crete. Moreover, Theseus had taken Princess Ariadne, King Minos' daughter, with him.

Next morning, when the King discovered what had happened, there was uproar throughout the entire palace. The first person the enraged King had called for was Daedalus, the craftsman who had made the labyrinth in which the Minotaur was kept.

"Where is that wretched Daedalus? Where is he?" King Minos raged. "I will tear him apart! I will burn him with hot coals! I will fling him off the cliff! The wretch, the liar! He told me that no one could get out of the labyrinth alive! Now the Minotaur is dead and Theseus has escaped with my hostages and my daughter!"

Daedalus heard the shouting and raving coming from the King's rooms and realised that the time had come to leave Crete – and to leave immediately! It was only a matter of time before Minos' soldiers came to arrest Daedalus – to drag him to the King.

Daedalus shook Icarus' shoulder again, more violently this time. Icarus opened his eyes and murmured sleepily, "What is it, Father? Why do I have to wake up now?"

"We have to escape, my son," Daedalus whispered urgently. "I will explain why later. But if we don't go now, it could mean death for both of us."

Icarus was wide awake now. His father was obviously worried, very worried indeed.

"You know you've always wanted to fly," Daedalus said. "Well, now's your chance."

Daedalus went over to a large box in the corner of the room. Somehow, Daedalus had always known that one day, he and Icarus might have to escape from Crete. So he had made wings from bird feathers, and set aside four balls of wax with which to stick them to their bodies.

Daedalus lifted the wings from the box and attached one pair on to Icarus' back. 'Poor Icarus,' Daedalus thought. 'He believes it's all a game.'

This was the second time he and his son had been forced to escape from danger together. The first time, Daedalus had to flee from his native city of Athens after he had thrown his nephew, Perdix, over a cliff in a fit of jealousy. Although Perdix was only a young boy, he was already a very clever inventor and craftsman. He was much cleverer, people said, than Daedalus himself. As Perdix tumbled over the cliff, the goddess Athene had saved him from death by turning him into a partridge.

Even so, Daedalus was afraid of what would happen when his crime was discovered, so he took Icarus and fled by night to the island of Crete. There, King Minos had given him shelter. Now Daedalus and Icarus had to run away again.

At last, Daedalus was satisfied with Icarus' wings. They were well fixed and should carry him safely across the sea. However, as Daedalus fixed his own larger wings on to his own back, he had a strong warning for Icarus.

"Remember your wings are stuck on with wax," Daedalus said. "Wax melts in heat, so take care not to fly too near the sun, or your wings will fall off! You understand, don't you, Icarus?"

"Oh yes, Father, of course I understand," Icarus replied, only half-listening.

Icarus was too excited at the thought of flying like a bird to think of anything else. The wings on his back were made of beautiful snow-white feathers, just like those of the birds he had often watched flying over the island. Already, Icarus felt very proud of them. With his great white wings, he would fly far better and further than his cousin Perdix, who had become a partridge. 'Partridges are only small, grey birds,' Icarus thought scornfully.

Daedalus looked at the eager, excited face of his son and prayed that no harm would befall him.

"Just follow me," he told Icarus. "Don't fly any higher than I do, and you will be all right!"

Just then, Daedalus heard a sound in the corridor outside. It was the tramp, tramp, tramp of soldiers' feet marching speedily towards his rooms.

"Quickly, Icarus!" Daedalus spoke urgently, as he led his son on to the balcony. "Jump up into the air when I tell you, and don't look down!" Daedalus gave Icarus a quick, anxious kiss, then said, "Now, Icarus! Jump!"

Icarus did as he was told and together with his father, he rose slowly into the air. The wings attached to his back moved up and down, and before long, Icarus and Daedalus were flying high above the grounds of the palace, over the golden sandy beaches along the shore and out to sea. The sun shone warm and bright around them, the sea below sparkled and the air felt fresh and clean on their faces as they flew along.

Every now and then, Daedalus looked round anxiously, to ensure Icarus was behind him. Every time, Icarus waved excitedly at his father. He was enjoying himself.

An hour or so passed. Below there was nothing to be seen but the sea and an occasional fishing boat. The island of Crete had long since disappeared below the horizon. By this time, Icarus was getting bored with just flying along behind his father. He wanted to do as the birds did – swoop downwards, turn and zoom upwards, perhaps move sideways in the wind currents that were blowing around him.

Icarus decided to try something. He glanced ahead to see that his father was not looking, then spread his wings out straight. He waggled them a little at the tips and found himself flying sideways.

"It works!" Icarus cried, in excitement.

Next, Icarus leaned downwards and swooped

for a second or two, then zoomed upwards again so that he was once more flying behind Daedalus. Now Icarus could almost believe that he had never been anything but a flying creature.

Just then, a flock of birds came zooming up, right in front of Icarus. They were making for greater heights, before levelling out again. Icarus followed them. Up, up he went, hardly noticing that it was becoming hotter and hotter as he got higher and higher. The sun was shining more and more brightly, but Icarus did not stop.

"I can fly as high as the birds," he said. "I know I can."

Suddenly, far below, Daedalus turned round again. He found the sky behind him was empty. Greatly alarmed, Daedalus looked up and saw to his horror, that Icarus was nothing but a small dot high in the sky.

"Icarus! Icarus!" Daedalus cried out in great fear. "Icarus, come back!"

Icarus was far too high to hear him. Besides, he was feeling rather faint from the heat of the sun. He also grew more and more frightened as the wind currents took hold of him and shot him upwards at tremendous speed. Suddenly Icarus felt two burning patches on his back. The wax! It was melting! Suddenly, instead of flying, Icarus was falling. Below him as he fell, he saw his two wings being thrown about by the wind. They had come off.

Down, down Icarus plunged, faster and faster. Daedalus was turning this way and that, trying to see where his son was. Suddenly, the boy fell past him, arms flailing wildly, hands trying to clutch at the air. Daedalus turned cold with fear and grief. He was helpless. All he could do was to watch Icarus falling away from him, getting smaller and smaller until a splash of foam in the sea below marked the spot where he plunged into the water.

"Icarus, my son, my son!" Daedalus moaned. A dreadful ache entered his heart, for he realised Icarus could not have survived such a long fall into the sea.

Tears began to stream from Daedalus' eyes. He knew he had to find Icarus.

It was all too clear to Daedalus that Icarus was dead, as he flew down close to the level of the sea. He found Icarus' limp body floating on the surface. His face was terribly white and his eyes were closed. Floating nearby were the wings which had fallen from his back.

The weeping Daedalus gently lifted Icarus out of the water. There was a small, rocky island not far away. Daedalus flew to it and landed on a small patch of sand on the shore. For a few moments, Daedalus was unable to do anything but hold Icarus close to him and weep. At last, though, Daedalus realised that Icarus would have to be buried. With a grieving heart, he began to cover his son with rocks and stones from the sea shore.

There were many birds on the island and a small group of them perched on a rock nearby, as if they were watching Daedalus. One of them suddenly chirruped and, looking up, Daedalus saw it was a partridge.

'A partridge!' thought Daedalus. He looked more closely at the grey bird and remembered how his nephew Perdix had been changed into a partridge by Athene. Perhaps this partridge, looking at him now, was Perdix.

"If you are," Daedalus wept, "you will see how my crime against you has been avenged."

Jason and the Golden Fleece

"So, Jason," said King Aeetes of Colchis. "You have come for the Golden Fleece!" Aeetes looked sternly at young Prince Jason of Iolcos, whose ship the 'Argo' had just sailed into the harbour at Colchis. "I must warn you that many have come before you, and all have failed. The dragon which guards the Fleece has killed every one of them!"

Aeetes hoped that Jason would be frightened by this warning. Some young warriors, who thought themselves very brave, had turned pale at the mention of the dragon. Others had found some excuse not to try to get the Fleece and very quickly left Colchis for home.

Jason was not like that. He had, in fact, solemnly sworn to fetch the Fleece and take it back with him to Iolcos. Only then would Jason's uncle, Pelias, keep his promise to give back the kingdom of Iolcos which he had stolen from Jason's father, King Aeson.

"I am not afraid, Your Majesty," Jason declared proudly. "I and my men, the Argonauts, have already braved many dangers to reach your land. We have faced huge giants, storms, winds and mighty waves at sea. The dragon which guards the Fleece cannot be more dangerous than these."

King Aeetes frowned. Jason was far too brave and confident for his liking. He was so brave and confident that he could well succeed where everyone else had failed.

The last thing Aeetes wanted was for Jason to take the Fleece. It was Aeetes' most precious possession. In any case, it belonged to Colchis and nowhere else. Many years ago, a prince called Phrixus had flown to Colchis on the back of a golden ram. After the ram died, Phrixus hung its fleece in the grove. He set a dragon to guard it, thinking the fearsome creature would keep the Golden Fleece safe from anyone who tried to take it.

Now Jason had arrived, it looked as if the Fleece was not so safe. Even so, King Aeetes was determined to keep it from him. So, he tried warning Jason again.

"The dragon never rests," he told the young Prince of Iolcos. "It watches the Fleece by day and by night."

"And I shall never rest," Jason answered, "until I get the Fleece from it."

Aeetes was furious at this reply, but he hid his feelings. Instead, he smiled and said, "If you are as brave in deed as you are in words, Jason, then the dragon will have much to fear. But come, let us talk no more of dragons and dangers. There will be plenty of time for that tomorrow. Now, you and your Argonauts must dine with me."

That night, King Aeetes was too worried to sleep. 'I must get rid of Jason,' he thought. 'I must think of a way to stop him taking the Fleece.'

All night, Aeetes walked back and forth, back and forth, in his bedchamber. All night, he plotted and schemed against Jason. Then at last, as dawn was breaking, Aeetes thought of a suitable plan.

"I'll give Jason three tasks," Aeetes decided. "Only after he has performed them all can he have the Golden Fleece!" Aeetes laughed out loud. "Jason will never perform the tasks," he chuckled with great glee. "They are all impossible! Each one is meant to kill him. He will be dead before he has finished the first – and the Fleece will be safe once again."

Unknown to King Aeetes, his daughter Medea knew of his wicked plans. Medea was a witch, with great powers. She was able to read her father's thoughts, even though her bedchamber in the palace was far away from his. What she learned greatly alarmed Medea.

She had fallen in love with Jason, even though she had never seen him before he arrived at the palace of Colchis the previous day.

"I must warn Jason," Medea decided. "With my magic, he can perform the tasks my father wants to set him. Without it, he will surely die!"

Medea hurried along the corridors of the palace to the room where Jason lay asleep. Without bothering to knock, Medea ran into the room and woke him up.

"Listen to me, Jason," she whispered urgently. "I have come to save your life!"

At that, Jason became very wide-awake.

"Who wishes to kill me?" he asked.

"My father, the King!" Medea replied, and briefly she told him of Aeetes' plans. The news made Jason very angry. He wanted to go and kill Aeetes there and then, before the treacherous King got the chance to kill him.

"No, no, Jason!" Medea told him. "I have a better way. Here – take this magic ointment. It will protect you while you perform the first task. For the second task, you will need this magic stone . . ."

"And for the third task?" Jason asked.

"Make sure your Argonaut, Orpheus is with you . . . and make sure he brings his lyre, the one that plays such beautiful music. Then the Golden Fleece will be yours," Medea said triumphantly.

Next morning, King Aeetes summoned Jason to his throne-room, and told him of the three tasks he had to perform.

"First," Aeetes instructed, "you must yoke two fire-breathing bulls to a plough and with them you must plough four acres of land. Next, you must sow the land with the teeth of dragons. A host of fierce armed men will at once grow from these teeth and you must kill them all!"

"I will do so!" Jason cried, pretending that he knew nothing of Aeetes' wickedness.

"Next," Aeetes went on, "you must kill the dragon in the magic grove. Only then can you take the Fleece home to Iolcos."

Shortly afterwards, a great crowd gathered in the fields outside the palace to watch Jason perform the first two tasks. King Aeetes was there and so was Medea. Apart from Medea, no one thought Jason had any hope of succeeding. Either the bulls would burn him up with their fiery breath or the host of armed men would kill him.

Jason came on to the field, clad in his finest armour. People in the crowd sighed and shook their heads, thinking what a pity it was that such a brave young warrior was soon going to die. What they did not know, of course, was that Jason had rubbed the magic ointment Medea had given him all over his body and his armour.

Suddenly, there was a great noise of hooves and the hiss of flames as two bulls came thundering into the field. Their eyes were fierce and with every breath, great blasts of fire leapt from their

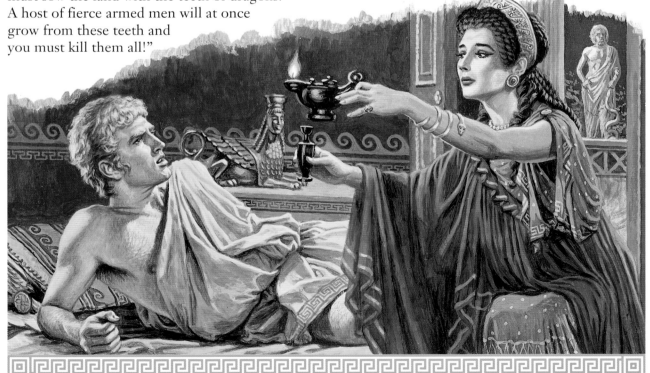

nostrils. Their hooves were made of white-hot metal and the ground steamed with heat as they trod on it.

'Soon, Jason will be burned to cinders!' thought King Aeetes gleefully as he watched Jason stride out towards the bulls. The next moment, though, Aeetes was glowering with anger as Jason marched into the flames quite unharmed. Because of Medea's ointment, he did not even feel the heat that surrounded him.

Jason grasped each of the bulls by one of its horns and with a quick movement, smashed their heads together. The animals fell to their knees dizzy and dazed. Quickly, Jason slipped a yoke over their heads, and waited for them to recover. When the bulls staggered to their feet, all their ferocity had gone and the fire in their nostrils and their hooves had cooled.

The bulls were now as meek as lambs, and they obediently pulled the plough across the four acres of land, with Jason directing from behind.

The crowd gasped in amazement at the sight. King Aeetes was furious. He wondered by what magic Jason had managed to perform this feat.

"Still, the next task will see the end of Jason," the King comforted himself.

Once again, though, Aeetes was disappointed and once again the watching crowd were amazed. Hundreds of armed men sprang from the dragons' teeth that Jason sowed. Jason hurled Medea's magic stone amongst them as she had told him. At once, the armed men turned on each other. They each accused the others of throwing the stone. They argued. They shouted. They began fighting among themselves. Soon, every one of them lay dead in the field from which they had grown only minutes before.

The crowd cheered and clapped and shouted

with pleasure. They soon fell silent, however, when King Aeetes jumped to his feet and in a loud and angry voice called out, "Enough! Two such great tasks are enough for one morning! You must rest, Jason."

"But Your Majesty . . ." Jason protested.

Trembling with rage and frustration, King Aeetes interrupted him. "No! I have said it is enough! You can attempt the third task to-morrow."

'Tomorrow, my brave Jason, you and all your Argonauts will be dead!' Aeetes thought as he stalked angrily to his palace. As soon as he got there, Aeetes summoned the commander of his soldiers. He ordered him to kill Jason and his Argonauts as they slept in their rooms that night.

Medea, of course, was listening. At once she rushed to Jason and told him of this latest treachery planned by her father.

"You must get the Golden Fleece tonight!" she urged him. "Tomorrow will be too late!"

That night, Jason crept silently from his room, woke the Argonaut, Orpheus and with him crept out to the magic grove.

They saw the grove long before they entered it. The Fleece, which hung from a tree, shone so brightly that it filled the surrounding woods with brilliant golden light. It was so bright, that to Jason it looked like another sun shining inside the grove. Beneath it, his eyes watchful and unsleeping, sat the dragon.

"This must be the most fearsome dragon in the world!" Jason whispered to Orpheus, looking at the creature's thick, spiky tail and mouth full of sharp teeth. "But come, Orpheus. Sing."

Orpheus plucked the strings on his lyre and began to sing the most beautiful melody. When it heard it, the dragon pricked up its ears and stared in the direction of the sound. The music was so beautiful that the dragon's eyes lost some of their fierce expression. Then, as Jason watched and Orpheus continued to sing, the dragon opened its huge mouth and yawned. Its eyelids began to blink. It felt sleepy for the first time in its life. Then, its eyes closed and the dragon slumped down on the ground, fast asleep.

"Keep on singing, Orpheus," Jason whispered. Quickly he ran across the floor of the grove, sword in hand. Jason gave one great swipe with his sword and cut through the neck of the sleeping dragon. Then he scrambled up the boughs of the tree and unhooked the glittering Fleece.

Orpheus helped Jason stuff the Fleece into a sack. They did not want its golden light to give them away. Then they ran back through the woods and down along the narrow, tree-lined paths that led to the harbour of Colchis.

There, Medea and the rest of the Argonauts were already waiting in the 'Argo'. Jason and Orpheus jumped on board. The ropes that held the ship to the quayside were cut and the Argonauts rowed swiftly and silently out of the harbour. The wind filled the 'Argo's' sails and by the time King Aeetes discovered what had happened, Jason, Medea and the Argonauts were far out to sea.

The triumphant Jason left one raging, furious King behind him in Colchis. Another King was just as furious when the 'Argo' brought Jason home to Iolcos.

Jason's uncle, King Pelias, had sent him to fetch the Golden Fleece believing the dragon who guarded it would kill him. Now that Jason had returned, Pelias was forced to keep his promise. He had to give back the Kingdom of Iolcos which he had stolen.

Once the wicked Pelias had gone, Jason brought back his father, King Aeson, from exile. It was a great day when Jason led his father to the throne in the palace of Iolcos, from which Pelias had driven him so many years before. That night there was a great feast to mark Jason's return and on the wall of the banqueting hall the Golden Fleece hung. It spread its brilliant light over a scene of great celebration.

Bellerophon
and Pegasus

"**I**t's Pegasus!" shouted Bellerophon.

At first, Bellerophon thought the reflection in the fountain was that of a huge white bird. When he looked up, he was thrilled to see it was a winged horse. It was the famous and beautiful Pegasus.

Bellerophon saw Pegasus glide down out of the sky on his silver wings. He landed on the bank near the fountain and began to drink. Bellerophon watched from his hiding place behind a nearby bush. In his hand, he held the magic golden bridle which the goddess Athene had given him.

"Pegasus is a wild horse," Athene explained. "No one has ever ridden on his back. But if you put this bridle on him, he will become tame."

Bellerophon had waited for Pegasus for many months. The winged horse did not come often to the fountain. Now Bellerophon could see the wait had been very worthwhile. With his powerful wings and strong back, Pegasus was a magnificent steed. He was the only horse strong and swift enough to carry Bellerophon in his great task of killing the monster, Chimaera.

Chimaera was a truly horrible creature. It had the head of a lion, the body of a goat and the tail of a serpent. It breathed fire and flames and for years it had been carrying off animals and small children. Chimaera's fiery breath burned down forests, fields of grain and whole villages and left them nothing but heaps of ashes.

Bellerophon had resolved to kill this dreadful monster, but he needed Pegasus to help him. First, though, he had to tame Pegasus. Bellerophon waited until the winged horse was chewing grass by the fountain. Then he ran swiftly towards him, took one great leap and landed on the horse's back. Pegasus was so alarmed that he launched himself into the sky at once. Up and up he went until he had taken Bellerophon above the clouds. Bellerophon clung on tightly all the way. Pegasus made tremendous efforts to dislodge him. He dived. He shot upwards again. He kicked his hind legs. He reared up. It was no use. Bellerophon remained firmly on his back.

Pegasus turned his head and tried to sink his teeth into Bellerophon's arm. That was when Bellerophon managed to slip the magic bridle over Pegasus' head and between his jaws. Just as Athene had said, Pegasus immediately became calm. He stopped throwing himself about the sky and now, when he looked at Bellerophon, all the wild fury had gone from his eyes. Instead, Pegasus gave his rider the look of an animal who knew and loved the man who was his master.

Bellerophon pressed his knees into Pegasus' sides. In response to this signal, the horse took him gliding down to the ground again. Bellerophon dismounted and went over to the spot where he had left the weapons with which he intended to kill Chimaera.

Then he climbed on to Pegasus' back once more and murmured, "Now, my splendid steed, let us seek Chimaera!"

It did not take long to find the monster. Bellerophon soon saw burnt and blackened fields below him.

'This is Chimaera's evil work,' he thought. 'The monster cannot be far away.'

Bellerophon saw it sitting on a mountain slope above the fields, grinning with satisfaction at the devastation it had caused.

"Chimaera has not seen us, Pegasus!" Bellerophon whispered. "We can surprise it. Now, my beauty, one of your swift, speedy dives – we must reach Chimaera quickly!"

Pegasus put his head down. As he swooped towards the Earth, Bellerophon held his bow firm and steady in one hand, and a bunch of arrows in the other.

"Slow down now, Pegasus," he whispered.

Pegasus obeyed and slowed down until he was hovering just above Chimaera's head. Swiftly, Bellerophon fitted the first of his arrows on to his bowstring.

Just then, Chimaera looked up. A terrible hatred and fury glittered in its eyes and the lion's mouth opened to let forth a huge blast of flame and smoke. The flames shot up, almost enveloping Bellerophon and Pegasus in scorching heat. It was now or never.

Bellerophon released the first arrow, snatched up another, placed it in the bowstring and released the string a second time. Again and again, the bowstring twanged and a deadly shower of arrows began to pour down upon Chimaera. Soon, the monster was festooned with arrows and shrieking in pain. As it shrieked, flames blasted out of its lion's mouth. In vain, Chimaera threshed about, trying to shake off the arrows. Then it raised its head and shot huge tongues of flame at Bellerophon.

Bellerophon released the last of the arrows and told Pegasus, "A little higher, my beautiful steed. I must be out of reach of Chimaera's fire while I prepare for my final attack."

Obediently, Pegasus beat his wings faster and lifted Bellerophon up into the air, away from Chimaera's shooting flames. Bellerophon reached down to where a bag hung from his saddle and pulled out a huge lump of lead. He placed the lead on the end of his spear and made sure it was firmly fixed.

Bellerophon looked down to where Chimaera was hurling itself about in fearful pain. He was waiting for the moment when the monster looked up and tried to reach him again with its blazing breath. Bellerophon watched closely. Then came the moment he was waiting for. The lion's head started to move up.

"Take me down, Pegasus!" Bellerophon shouted.

Just as Pegasus reached the right spot above Chimaera, its head lifted up and its huge mouth opened. At once, Bellerophon plunged his spear deep into Chimaera's mouth. There was a ghastly sizzling and boiling sound from inside the monster's jaws. The monster gave a fearful, shrieking howl that pierced Bellerophon's ears.

"The lead's melting!" Bellerophon cried triumphantly.

He pulled his spear out and saw that the lump of lead had gone. The fire in Chimaera's mouth was so great that it had melted the metal. In dreadful agony, Chimaera rolled on to the ground and threw itself about as the lead flowed down its throat and burned its insides away. The monster's shrieks and howls got louder and louder, until at last, it gave one final shudder and lay still. Smoke began to rise from its dead body. Before long, fire broke through its hide and Chimaera was enveloped in a blanket of flame. The fire burned for a long time. Afterwards, all that was left was a pile of black, smoking ashes.

Bellerophon was thrilled at his tremendous triumph, but one thing spoiled his joy. Now Chimaera was dead, Bellerophon would have to set Pegasus free. They had faced great danger together and Bellerophon had come to love the beautiful winged horse.

Bellerophon felt so sad when he removed the magic bridle and told Pegasus, "Now you can roam the skies as freely as you did before."

Pegasus did not move.

"You are free," Bellerophon repeated. But instead of flying away into the sky, as Bellerophon expected, Pegasus came to him and brushed his mane against his shoulder. Bellerophon was delighted. He knew what the winged horse was trying to say.

Pegasus did not want his freedom. He wanted to stay with his master – and of his own free will.

Perseus
and the
Gorgon

King Polydectes of Seriphos was feeling very pleased with himself. At last, he had managed to get rid of Perseus. The boy was a nuisance. Ever since he and his mother Danae had been shipwrecked on Seriphos, Perseus had protected her against the King. Polydectes, who hated both of them, wanted Danae as his slave. Determined to have his way, the King had tried for years to find some means of sending Perseus to certain death. Now he had succeeded.

"Perseus is a fool!" Polydectes laughed with wicked satisfaction. "He fell straight into my trap."

Polydectes' trap was simple. He invited Perseus to a banquet. The guests were supposed to bring some rich gift with them, but Perseus was so poor that he had nothing to give.

"You must wipe out this insult, Perseus!" Polydectes demanded, pretending to be very angry. "You must bring me the head of the Gorgon, Medusa! Swear you will do so!"

Perseus had to do as the King demanded. However, the task he swore to perform was not only difficult – it was impossible!

"Perseus cannot kill Medusa without looking directly at her," Polydectes chortled gleefully. "The moment he does so, he will be turned to stone!"

While King Polydectes was congratulating himself on his cleverness, Perseus was feeling desperate.

'What am I to do?' he thought. 'I don't want to be turned to stone but I can't kill Medusa with my eyes shut!' Perseus knew now that the King wanted him dead, but he could not go back on his word. That would be a dreadful disgrace.

"I am doomed," Perseus decided gloomily. "There is no escape!"

Happily, Perseus was wrong. The Greek gods Athene and Hermes had seen and heard all that had happened. They were watching from the Palace of Olympus where the gods lived high up in the clouds.

"Perseus is in terrible trouble," sighed Athene, the goddess of wisdom. "We must help him."

"Of course we must," replied Hermes, the messenger of the gods.

Hermes thought for several moments. Then at last he cried, "I've got it! Come, Athene, bring your shield which shines like a mirror. I'll bring my curved sword and a pair of my winged sandals."

"Where are we going?" asked Athene.

"To see Perseus," Hermes told her. "On the way we will call on Hades in the Underworld, and borrow his helmet of invisibility. Then we will go to the Nymphs and borrow their magic wallet. Come, Athene, we must hurry. There is no time to lose."

Suddenly, or so it seemed to Perseus, a bright, golden light started shining in front of him. Perseus was dazzled by it. Gradually, he was able to make out the shapes of the tall, beautiful Athene and the small, slim Hermes.

"Who are you?" Perseus asked, mystified by these creatures who shone with golden light.

"We are beings with great powers," said Athene. "We can do things humans find impossible."

"Like killing Medusa," Hermes added, with a smile. "Or at least telling you how it can be done!"

Perseus frowned. "You are making fun of me," he said suspiciously. "No one can kill Medusa without being turned to stone first!"

"You are wrong, Perseus! You can do it," replied Hermes cheerfully. "Here are the things you will need."

Perseus stared in amazement as Athene and Hermes laid before him Athene's shield, the helmet of invisibility, the magic wallet and Hermes' curved sword and winged sandals. "What use are all these things?" Perseus asked.

"Listen!" replied Hermes. The wings on his sandals flapped as he flew up to whisper in Perseus' ear. As Perseus listened to Hermes, he stopped frowning with worry. By the time Hermes had finished, Perseus was very cheerful and excited.

"Marvellous! Wonderful!" he cried, as Hermes fluttered back to the ground. "Now I can kill Medusa and get her head!"

"All you need to know now is the way to the Land of the Dead where Medusa and her two sisters live," said Athene.

"Don't you know it?" Perseus asked in surprise.

"Only the Old Grey Women have that knowledge," Hermes told him. "They are strange creatures with only one eye between them, but it is so powerful that it can see to the end of the world."

"What are we waiting for?" Perseus cried impatiently. "Let's go and ask them!"

Hermes put his hands under Perseus' elbow. Slowly, Perseus felt himself rise into the air. The wings on his own sandals were beating up and down like the wings of a bird. Perseus had never flown before and at first he wobbled a bit. Soon though, he was flying as swiftly and as surely as Hermes.

A few moments later, they were flying over a seashore and Hermes was pointing to a large cave close by the beach.

"There they are!" Hermes cried.

Perseus looked down and saw the three Old Grey Women coming out of the cave. Together with Hermes, he swooped downwards to land on the shore. At once, Hermes darted behind a nearby bush and signalled Perseus to do the same.

As the Old Grey Women approached, they were arguing fiercely.

"You've had the eye long enough now, Sister," croaked one Old Woman. "Let me have it. I want to take a look at the world."

"No, it's my turn," protested the Woman behind her.

The two blind Women were groping about, but the one with the eye avoided them. "You will both have to wait," she said. "I haven't finished with the eye yet."

"They always quarrel like this," Hermes whispered. "Wait until the Old Woman with the eye gives it to one of the others. Then all three are blind. Here's what you must do . . ."

Perseus waited until the Woman with the eye took it from the hole in the centre of her head and began passing it to one of her sisters.

"Now! Quick!" cried Hermes.

Perseus leapt up, rushed over to the Women and snatched up the eye. The Women shrieked with alarm.

"Who's there?" they cried. "Someone's stolen our eye!"

"Your eye is quite safe," said Perseus. "I have it here!"

"Give it back! Give it back this instant!"

"Not until you have told me how to reach the place where the Gorgons live!" Perseus said firmly.

The Old Grey Women whined and complained, but they knew that without their eye, they were all helpless. At last, they gave in. One of the Old Women angrily told Perseus all he wanted to know.

"Now," snarled the Old Woman when she had finished. "Give us back our eye!"

Perseus placed the eye in the forehead of the Old Woman who had spoken to him. As soon as she could see again, she tried to scratch him with her long, black fingernails. Perseus escaped by rising swiftly into the air on his winged sandals. Hermes went with him.

"We must part here," Hermes said. "Farewell, Perseus. Remember all you must do when you reach the land of the Gorgons."

Hermes soared into the clouds and out of sight. Perseus turned westwards, as the Old Women had said and flew past all the coasts and oceans which they told him led to his destination.

Beneath him as he flew, the Earth looked like a carpet of many colours. There was the dark green of the forests and grasslands. There was the gold of the sand on the seashore, and the blue of the lakes, rivers and oceans.

After a while, though, Perseus could see only black rocks and grey barren mountains. Perseus knew he was nearing his destination. At last, he saw a large, black island below. Three shapes lay on the rocks by the shore. They looked like giant, winged dragons.

"The Gorgons!" Perseus cried, feeling frightened and excited at the same time.

All three looked as if they were asleep. When he looked at them. Perseus shivered with horror.

The Gorgons were the most horrible creatures he had ever seen. From their cheeks grew two white tusks. Their hands had long claws made of brass. Two Gorgons were covered in dragon scales from head to toe. The head of the third Gorgon, instead of hair, was a mass of writhing snakes.

"That must be Medusa," breathed Perseus.

He had to hurry. The Gorgons might wake at any moment. Perseus hovered in the air, while he placed the helmet of invisibility on his head. He opened the magic wallet that hung from his belt and gripped Hermes' curved sword in his right hand. Then, with his left hand, Perseus carefully moved Athene's mirror-like shield until he could see Medusa's reflection in it.

Slowly, Perseus flew down towards the rock where Medusa lay, keeping her reflection in the shield all the time. He was nearly there – lower, then a little lower. Perseus was above Medusa's head.

'Now!' he thought, and with one swift stroke, he brought the curved sword down. Its tip clanged on the rock as it sliced through Medusa's neck. Perseus darted downwards, using the shield like a mirror to show him what to do. Quickly, Perseus grasped Medusa's head and pulled it off the sand where it had fallen. He pushed it into the wallet and fastened it tightly.

Just then, the other two Gorgons woke up. When they saw Medusa's headless body lying on the rock, they let out dreadful screams and howls. But they could not see who had killed her. The helmet of invisibility Perseus was wearing made sure of that.

It was time to escape. The wings of Perseus' sandals beat rapidly and he soared up into the air, leaving the two Gorgons screaming and clutching vainly at the air.

Perseus began his long journey back to the island of Seriphos. At last he flew down to land on the beach near Polydectes' palace.

A few minutes later, Perseus marched into the palace. Before anyone could stop him, he threw back the doors of the banquet hall, where Polydectes was feasting with his nobles. Everyone jumped in surprise.

When Polydectes saw that Perseus had returned, he went pale with fear.

"I have the Gorgon's head, Polydectes," Perseus said in a confident voice. "I have done as I promised."

Despite his fear, Polydectes laughed. "Come, now, Perseus!" he said. "How could you have killed Medusa and returned alive?"

By now the nobles of Seriphos had also recovered from their surprise.

"You lie, Perseus!"

"You're talking nonsense!"

"It is impossible!" These cries rang out from all around the hall.

Then Polydectes signalled to one of his servants. "Go, fetch the mother of this foolish boy!" the King instucted. "Bring Danae and let her see her son is a liar!"

When Danae entered the hall, Perseus found it hard to recognise her. Polydectes had forced her to do all the dirty jobs in the palace kitchens. She looked old and worn.

When she saw Perseus, Danae's eye shone with tears of joy. But Perseus was horrified to see how the King had ill-treated her.

"Keep your eyes on the floor, Mother," Perseus whispered to Danae. "Don't look at what I am going to do!"

Danae did as Perseus told her. Then Perseus turned again to King Polydectes. "You want proof that I have killed Medusa?" he demanded.

"You haven't any proof!" cried Polydectes.

"Very well, look at this!" Perseus replied and pulled Medusa's head out of the magic wallet.

Immediately, King Polydectes and his nobles turned into stone. Some had their mouths open in amazement. Others were holding up their hands to shield themselves from Medusa's terrible eyes. It was no use. They all became solid grey stone in an instant.

Perseus plunged Medusa's head back into the wallet and closed it. He put his arms round Danae and embraced her. She was gasping with amazement at the hall full of statues.

"We are free from the wicked King," Perseus told her. "He will never trouble anyone ever again!"

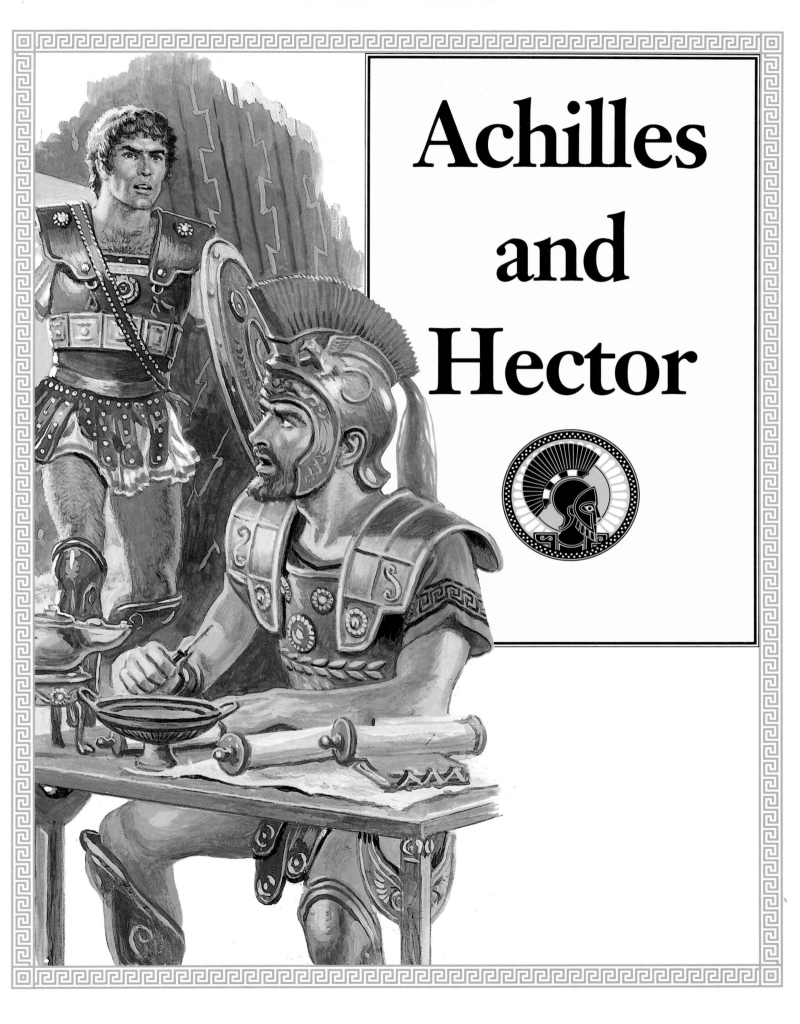

Achilles
and
Hector

"Achilles! Achilles! Come quickly!" Patroclus was shouting loudly as he ran through the Greek camp. He had dreadful news. The Trojans were attacking the Greek ships and throwing burning torches on to the decks. Dozens of Greeks had already been killed.

If Achilles had been there to fight them, the Trojans would not have dared to be this bold. However, Achilles was not there. After his quarrel with Agamemnon, the Greek leader, he had refused to fight and retired to his tent.

Achilles looked up, startled, when Patroclus burst into his tent. "Our ships and our men are in terrible danger," panted Patroclus. "You must save them, Achilles."

Briefly, Patroclus told Achilles what had happened. Then he added: "We have not fought Troy for nine years to lose the war now! Only you can save us."

"No," growled Achilles. "I will not come!"

"But Achilles . . ." Patroclus protested.

"Agamemnon insulted me," Achilles said gruffly. "I will not help him now!"

Patroclus fell to his knees in despair. "Then all is lost," he moaned.

Since Achilles had retired to his tent to sulk about Agamemnon, many Greeks had come to him begging him to return to the fight. Achilles had refused them all. He found it hard, though, to turn Patroclus away as roughly as he turned away the others. For Patroclus was his dearest friend. They were like brothers. So, when Achilles saw Patroclus weep in despair, he gave in just a little.

"I will not fight, Patroclus," Achilles repeated. "But I will help."

"How?" cried Patroclus, suddenly hopeful again.

"I will lend you my armour," Achilles told him. "When the Trojans see it, they will think I have rejoined our men."

This was marvellous news. The Trojans feared Achilles more than any other warrior on Earth.

Quickly, Achilles helped Patroclus buckle on his shining armour. Patroclus felt proud to be wearing it.

Achilles, however, had two warnings for him. "If you succeed in driving the Trojans away from our ships, do not pursue them back to Troy. And keep away from Hector!" Achilles added sternly. "He is the greatest of the Trojan warriors. Only I can match him in battle."

"I will remember," Patroclus promised.

"Make haste, then, and may the gods protect you, dearest friend," Achilles said.

Riding in Achilles' chariot, Patroclus sped back to the battlefield. He arrived to find the fighting was more savage than ever. The sky overhead was black with smoke from the burning Greek ships. The shore was littered with the bodies of dead Greeks and their upturned chariots. The air was filled with the ringing sounds of swords clashing with spears, and the shouts and cries of men locked in fierce contest.

However, when the Trojans saw Patroclus disguised in Achilles' armour, they became terrified. They broke off the fight and began speeding their chariots towards their city of Troy and safety.

"After them! After them!" cried Patroclus. He was so excited, he forgot Achilles' warning.

Patroclus and the Greeks set off at tremendous speed. Their chariots threw up clouds of dust as they chased the fleeing Trojans. They drove so

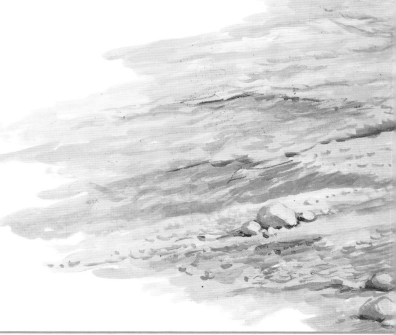

fast that when they came within sight of Troy, the Trojans were still some distance from the city.

"We're catching up!" Patroclus cried in triumph.

Just then, a Trojan turned his chariot round and began driving back towards Patroclus. Patroclus recognised him at once.

"It's Hector!" he gasped. It was too late. Patroclus remembered Achilles' second warning. Frightened, Patroclus flung his spear at Hector's chariot. It missed.

When the rest of the Greeks saw Hector's chariot thundering towards them, they loosed a shower of arrows. They failed to stop him. Hector drove straight at Patroclus and with one blow struck him on the side of the neck with his sword. Achilles' armour stopped the blow from killing Patroclus, but his helmet and neckplate were knocked to the ground.

Hector was surprised to see Patroclus' face. "You are not Achilles!" he cried, and before Patroclus could move, Hector plunged his spear into his unprotected throat. Patroclus died instantly. His body tumbled off the chariot into the dust. Hector jumped down, and began pulling off Achilles' shining armour.

When Achilles learned that Patroclus was dead, he gave a terrible howl of grief. He was so overcome with sorrow that he fell to the floor of his tent. He pounded the earth with his fists. He sobbed. He cried out his friend's name. He wept again and vowed to get his revenge.

"Hector!" Achilles suddenly shouted in a thunderous voice, as if to make the Trojan warrior hear him. "You shall die! And after death, you shall be punished."

That night, Achilles did not sleep. He could think of only one thing: he must kill Hector and avenge his lifelong friend Patroclus. Hector also remained awake. He knew that when he met Achilles it would be in the most savage battle he had ever fought.

That night Hephaestus, the god of fire and industry, was busy making Achilles a fresh suit of armour to wear in his battle with Hector.

Next morning, Achilles found the armour in his tent. He put it on and came out, fully armed and armoured for battle. The Greeks were very pleased to see that Achilles had at last returned to fight by their side.

When the fighting started that day, Achilles fought like a madman.

After a few hours, the Greeks could no longer count the number of Trojans Achilles had killed.

All the time, Achilles was looking for Hector. It was late in the afternoon before he saw him. By that time, the Greeks had fought their way up to the walls of Troy. The Trojan warriors were rushing back into the city and guards stood ready to close the gates as soon as they were all inside.

Hector, however, refused to come in. He stood outside the gates, waiting for Achilles. His father, King Priam, came on to the battlements and begged Hector to seek safety within the walls of Troy. Hector's mother, Hecuba, and his wife Andromache, also came and pleaded with Hector. Hector would not listen.

Then Hector saw a great flash of brilliant light not far away. The last rays of the afternoon sun had struck Achilles' brilliant armour. Nearer and nearer it came, until Achilles could be seen thundering towards Hector in his chariot at tremendous speed. There was a terrible look of hatred on Achilles' face as he saw Hector.

Achilles' chariot swept towards the waiting Hector, and as it came close, Hector threw his spear. Achilles saw it coming, and raised his shield. The spear hit it, bounced off and clattered to the ground. At once, Hector drew his sword and came rushing towards Achilles. Achilles jumped from his chariot and sprang towards him, with his spear outstretched.

"Die as Patroclus died, vile Trojan!" Achilles snarled. His spearhead went through Hector's neck. With a dreadful choking sound, Hector fell to the ground, dead.

There was a cry of horror from the battlements above as Priam, Hecuba and Andromache saw Hector fall. But their horror and grief grew even greater when they saw what happened next.

Achilles took his dagger and cut though Hector's feet from the heels to the ankles. He pushed a rope through the holes and fastened the end of it to his chariot. Then Achilles leapt into his chariot, whipped the horses into a gallop and began dragging Hector across the ground. Faster and faster the chariot went with Hector's body trailing behind it. Soon the body was torn, battered and black with dust.

Each day for many days after that, Achilles returned to the walls of Troy with Hector's dead body trailing behind his chariot. Day after day, King Priam wept bitterly at the dreadful spectacle.

At last, Priam could bear the sight no longer.

'I must forget I am a King, and humble myself before Achilles,' he thought.

The grief-stricken Priam left Troy and went to the Greek camp, taking with him many magnificent gifts. The gifts would be Hector's ransom, or so Priam hoped. When he entered Achilles' tent, Priam threw himself before the great Greek warrior.

"Have pity on me!" Priam wept. "Have pity, great Achilles! Give me back my dead son."

For a while Achilles said nothing. He seemed stern and unyielding. Priam pleaded with him again. He even kissed Achilles' hands, which is what servants did to show obedience to their masters.

At this, Achilles looked down at Priam's lined, old face and his sorrowful eyes, which were swollen and red with weeping. Suddenly, Achilles remembered his own father, Peleus.

'If Hector had killed me,' Achilles thought, 'my father would have wept for me in the same way.'

The remembrance of his own father made Achilles take pity on Priam at last.

"Do not kneel to me, old man!" he said. "Do not weep! The body of your son shall be washed and clothed, and you shall return with it to Troy."

Achilles kept his word. Priam received the body of Hector and took it home to be properly buried.

As he watched Priam leave, Achilles knew that the gods on Olympus would punish him for the dishonourable deed he had committed. He knew, too, what the punishment would be.

'I shall be killed here, at Troy,' Achilles thought. 'I shall never return home to my father, and he will not be able to bury my body, as Priam will bury Hector's.'

Not long afterwards, all this came true. Achilles was killed by Paris, Hector's younger brother, and his father never saw him again.

Horatius at the Bridge

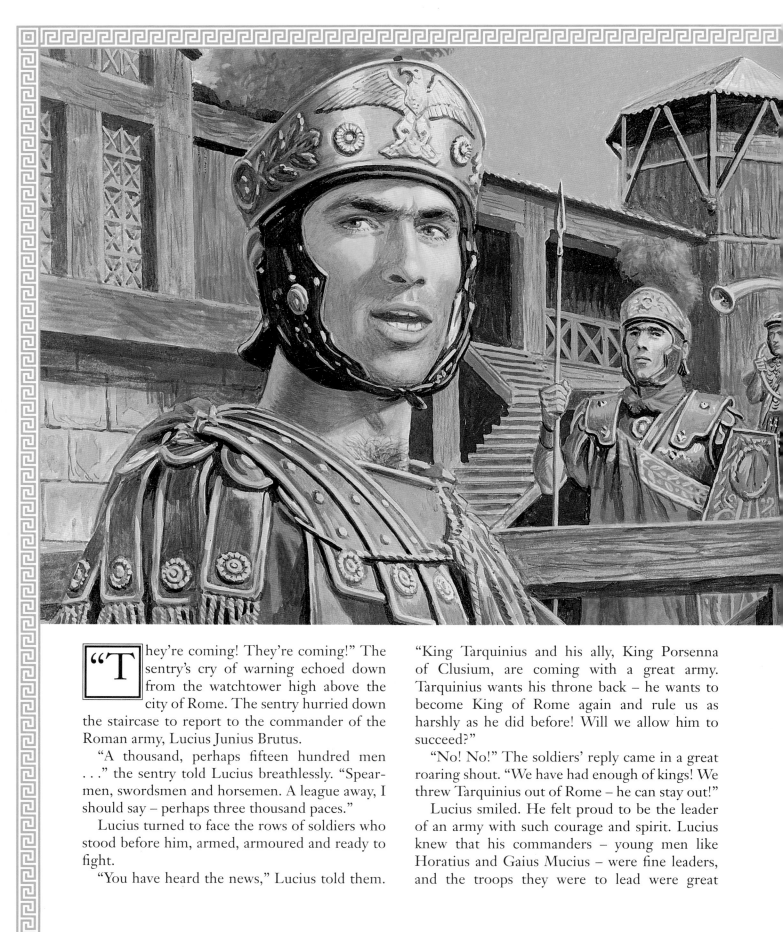

"They're coming! They're coming!" The sentry's cry of warning echoed down from the watchtower high above the city of Rome. The sentry hurried down the staircase to report to the commander of the Roman army, Lucius Junius Brutus.

"A thousand, perhaps fifteen hundred men . . ." the sentry told Lucius breathlessly. "Spearmen, swordsmen and horsemen. A league away, I should say – perhaps three thousand paces."

Lucius turned to face the rows of soldiers who stood before him, armed, armoured and ready to fight.

"You have heard the news," Lucius told them.

"King Tarquinius and his ally, King Porsenna of Clusium, are coming with a great army. Tarquinius wants his throne back – he wants to become King of Rome again and rule us as harshly as he did before! Will we allow him to succeed?"

"No! No!" The soldiers' reply came in a great roaring shout. "We have had enough of kings! We threw Tarquinius out of Rome – he can stay out!"

Lucius smiled. He felt proud to be the leader of an army with such courage and spirit. Lucius knew that his commanders – young men like Horatius and Gaius Mucius – were fine leaders, and the troops they were to lead were great

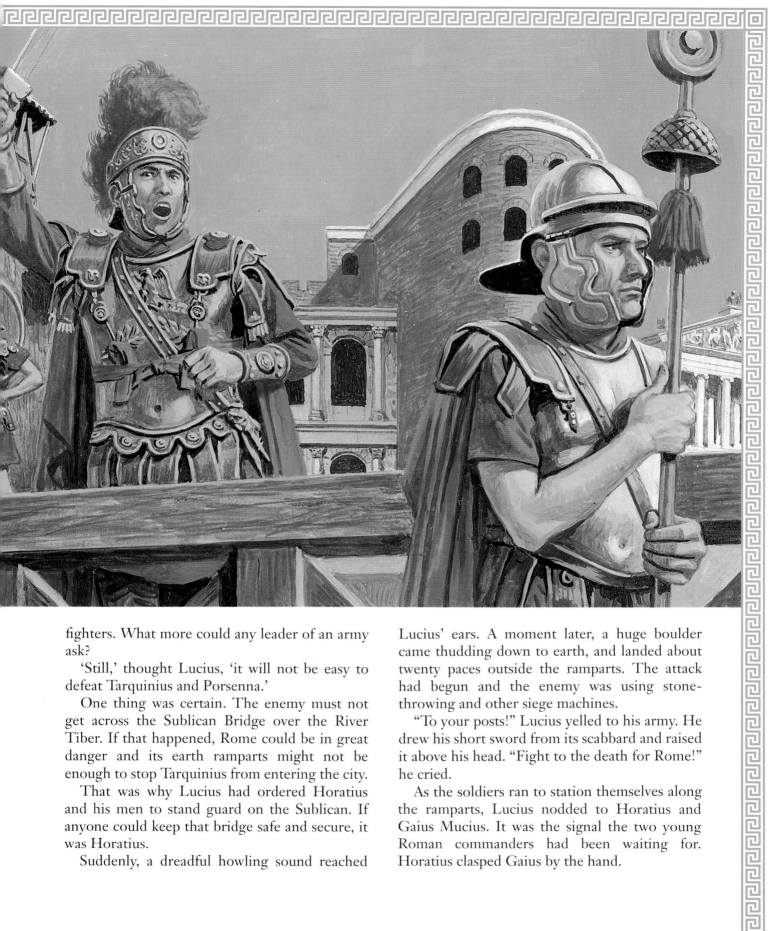

fighters. What more could any leader of an army ask?

'Still,' thought Lucius, 'it will not be easy to defeat Tarquinius and Porsenna.'

One thing was certain. The enemy must not get across the Sublican Bridge over the River Tiber. If that happened, Rome could be in great danger and its earth ramparts might not be enough to stop Tarquinius from entering the city.

That was why Lucius had ordered Horatius and his men to stand guard on the Sublican. If anyone could keep that bridge safe and secure, it was Horatius.

Suddenly, a dreadful howling sound reached Lucius' ears. A moment later, a huge boulder came thudding down to earth, and landed about twenty paces outside the ramparts. The attack had begun and the enemy was using stone-throwing and other siege machines.

"To your posts!" Lucius yelled to his army. He drew his short sword from its scabbard and raised it above his head. "Fight to the death for Rome!" he cried.

As the soldiers ran to station themselves along the ramparts, Lucius nodded to Horatius and Gaius Mucius. It was the signal the two young Roman commanders had been waiting for. Horatius clasped Gaius by the hand.

"Death to Tarquinius!" Horatius said firmly. "The gods preserve you, Gaius, my friend!"

"The gods preserve you, Horatius," Gaius replied. "You greatly need their protection."

Gaius was right, Horatius thought, as he led his fifty men out of the city, and down the Palatine Hill towards the Tiber and the Sublican Bridge. The gods of Rome would have to fight very hard on his side, for defending the bridge was a truly perilous task. It had no proper defences. All Horatius and his men could do was to stand and fight with the River Tiber and the bridge behind them.

The bridge was made of thick, strong wooden planks. Many times since it was first built by Ancius, fourth King of Rome, the bridge had been swept away by floods. This was not one of those times, however. The Sublican stood strong and firm as Horatius marched across, and the river flowed quietly beneath it.

"Spearmen, over there – swordsmen on this side!" Horatius quickly ordered his men to their positions. He concentrated half his force at the end of the bridge, and stationed the rest along the banks of the river on either side.

The army of Tarquinius and Porsenna was very close now, so close that Horatius could see the designs emblazoned on their shields. Horatius tried to count the number of enemy soldiers, but there were too many of them.

Suddenly, Horatius heard the whistling sound of a spear slicing through the air towards him. He jumped aside to avoid it and the spearhead struck the bridge and stuck there. A swordsman was making straight for him, yelling fearful war cries and brandishing his sword in the air. Horatius leapt forward, thrusting his own sword up and the two swords met with a loud metallic

clang. There came a scraping sound as the swordsman whipped his sword away. He wielded it again to strike another blow at Horatius, but before he could do so Horatius lunged forward and plunged his sword into the man's chest. The man gave a horrible gurgling cry and crumpled to the ground.

Quickly, Horatius looked round. Along the bank of the river, fierce struggles were going on, with two enemy soldiers or more lunging at each Roman with swords and spears.

The air was filled with the sounds and the screams of battle, the clash of sword on sword, the whistle of javelins flying through the air and, from some distance in front of Horatius, the heavy clank and thud of the enemy's siege machines. Several times, Horatius saw huge boulders and stones flying through the air above his head. The boulders fell into the river behind him, but Horatius realised what the enemy was trying to do.

'They're trying to kill us all quickly – one of those boulders could crush five men,' Horatius thought anxiously.

For the moment, the aim of the men working the siege machines was not accurate. All their missiles fell into the Tiber or on to the opposite bank of the river.

If they shortened their range a bit or pulled their siege machines back a little . . .

Then it happened. A great boulder came whistling over and hit its target – half a dozen of Horatius' spearmen who were holding a group of enemy soldiers at bay with their javelins. There was a dreadful crash and terrible screams as the spearmen were crushed down onto the ground by the enormous weight.

Suddenly, Horatius smelled burning. He looked quickly along the river bank. Several Romans, their clothing ablaze, were leaping into the water in an attempt to put out the flames. It was obvious what had happened. The siege machines were now being used to fling burning torches.

Then Horatius saw something even more horrifying. Not one of his fifty men was left standing. Their bodies were strewn on the ground, floating in the river or sprawled out on the banks sloping down to the water.

Horatius was alone – the only man left out of his entire force!

"Very well, then!" Horatius cried. "If that's how the gods have decreed, I'll defend the bridge alone!"

Horatius snatched up a javelin lying nearby, and leapt a few paces back along the bridge. There he stood, sword in one hand, javelin in the other, with his shield looped firmly round one arm. Horatius snarled at the crowd of enemy soldiers in front of him. "But that one man is a Roman! You shall not cross this bridge, I swear it!"

The enemy soldiers were so startled that for a moment they did not move. Then one of them began to laugh.

"He's mad!" he yelled. "Imagine one man against all of us!"

Other soldiers took up the cry and started to yell insults at Horatius. "You're a lunatic!" they shouted. "You'd best jump in the river and cool your crazy head!"

Horatius stood his ground, his eyes dark with fury and determination. "You shall not cross!" he growled. He lunged at one enemy soldier who was just about to jump on to the bridge in front of him. The enemy retreated hastily, back to the safety of the crowd at the end of the bridge.

Horatius realised that the soldiers were afraid of him. They thought he was out of his mind, and feared to fight against a madman. It could not go on for much longer though. Someone would throw a spear or a sword, and that would be the end.

Fortunately, Gaius Mucius had seen what was happening from the ramparts above. He ordered his men to open the gates so that they could go to Horatius' aid.

"Fetch some axes!" Gaius ordered. "There's only one way to save Horatius – and Rome. We've got to chop that bridge down."

Horatius' position was getting very dangerous now. As Gaius and his men rushed out of the gates and started running down towards the bridge, one of the enemy soldiers lunged at Horatius with his sword. Horatius managed to twist the sword out of the man's hand and throw him back. Gaius knew it would only take seconds

for Horatius to be overwhelmed, if the enemy came at him in force.

Reaching the bridge, Gaius started to hack away at the planks that held it to the river bank. Four or five others were doing the same. Gradually, the planks were cracking and splitting apart. Horatius felt the bridge vibrate and as the first four planks were chopped through, the whole bridge began to sway. The enemy soliders saw what was happening and drew back from their end of the bridge, fearful of being thrown into the water when it collapsed.

Gaius and his men kept chopping away at the planks, turning the blades of the axes to split the wood, until only one plank was left. By now, the bridge was swaying alarmingly. Gaius gave a terrific swipe with his axe and as the blade chopped through the last plank, the bridge suddenly tipped sideways. With a great creaking, groaning and splintering it toppled down towards the river. Horatius was flung off. He plunged into the water and disappeared, weighed down by his heavy armour. For one dreadful moment, Gaius thought Horatius had drowned. Then suddenly, there he was, up on the surface

again and swimming strongly towards the river bank. Gaius rushed forward and grabbing Horatius' hand, hauled him out of the water.

"There," Horatius told Gaius, pointing to the confused horde of enemy soldiers who were staring at the wrecked bridge. "I told them they wouldn't get across."

All along the ramparts, the Romans were cheering and shouting out Horatius' name. When he came back into the city, Lucius Junius Brutus was there to congratulate him for his magnificent deed. Lucius placed a laurel wreath on Horatius' head and told him, "This is the mark of a hero of Rome. You will be among Rome's greatest heroes, Horatius. Tarquinius will never come back now that he has Romans like you to contend with."

Lucius was right. After seeing what happened at the Sublican Bridge, King Porsenna, Tarquinius' ally, became afraid to fight against the Romans. Porsenna went home to Clusium, leaving Tarquinius with no soldiers to fight for him.

Tarquinius had lost his throne for ever, and never again were the Romans ruled by Kings.

Androclus and the Lion

Androclus shivered as another icy drop of water dripped on to his face. He looked up at the cave roof above his head. Another drop plopped down on to the rocky shelf beside him.

Androclus drew his cloak round his shoulders and wrapped his arms round himself trying to keep warm.

It was no use trying to sleep in this cave, he thought miserably. At least the soldiers who were out hunting for him would not find him in here, and maybe the lions would not find him either. Well, Androclus hoped so. The last thing he wanted was for a ferocious lion to come into the cave. The animal would probably be hungry, and then . . . Androclus did not want to think about what would happen.

'At least I'm free now,' Androclus thought, trying to cheer himself up.

One thing he knew for certain – his cruel master, Publius Sirius, would not be able to give him a beating today and then send him off, sore and aching, to do a day's hard labour in his vineyards. Androclus had hated his master ever since the day Publius had bought him in the slave market in Rome.

Four years passed before Androclus managed to escape from Publius' farm. Now, hiding inside the cave, Androclus thought over the plans he had made to get away from Italy. He would stay in the cave until it grew dark. The soldiers Publius had sent to catch him would not be looking for him at night. Then Androclus planned to leave the cave and make his way to the coast. There, he hoped to find a boat and sail back to his home in Greece.

Androclus looked at the shafts of light that were coming into the cave. The sun seemed to be low in the sky now. It might be dark soon.

"I must have a look," Androclus murmured. He peered out of the cave entrance. "Good," he said seeing the deep blue of the sky. "An hour or so, and the sun will set."

Suddenly, as he was turning to go back into the cave, Androclus saw the lion. His skin prickled with fright. He gave a start as a low, growling roar came from the lion's throat. It stood only a few metres away from him. It was a powerful creature, with a flowing mane and a great swishing tail. There was something strange, though. Surely the lion would have noticed Androclus by now?

However, it seemed to be more concerned with its front paw, which it was holding off the ground and licking from time to time. Every now and then, the lion gave a sort of whining howl, as if it was in pain.

When Androclus looked at the paw, he saw why. It was very swollen and rather black in colour. Quite obviously, it hurt a great deal. Androclus felt great pity for the wounded creature. He wanted to help, but it was a great risk.

Androclus was very soft-hearted. He loved animals and could not bear to see even a fierce lion suffering. His mind was made up quickly. Moving carefully, Androclus approached the lion. The lion was sitting down now, whining and licking its paw. As it heard Androclus creep closer, it looked up. Androclus saw that instead of the wild, ferocious glare lions usually had, this one was looking at him pleadingly, as if it wanted help.

Very slowly, Androclus stretched out his hand and stroked the lion's mane. To his relief, the lion let him do it.

"That's a bad paw you've got there, poor old fellow," Androclus murmured. "Let's have a look at it – all right, I won't hurt you!"

The lion gave a howl as Androclus touched its paw. For one terrible moment, Androclus thought it was going to attack him. But it looked sadly at Androclus and the howl became a whine. Androclus carefully lifted the lion's front leg and looked closely at the injured paw.

There was a large, sharp spike embedded in one of the pads. It looked like a large thorn, or a piece of metal.

"That's got to come out," said Androclus. It was best to do it quickly. Androclus grabbed the spike and pulled hard. As he did so, the lion gave a deafening roar.

Androclus went back into the cave to fetch some water from one of the many puddles that lay on the floor inside. Androclus tore his cloak into two long strips, soaked them in the ice-cold water and went outside again.

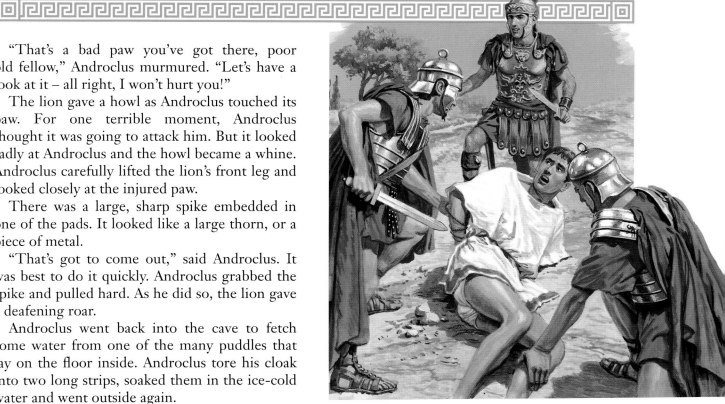

For the next few minutes Androclus bathed the swollen paw and wrapped it up in the long, wet strips of cloth. All the time, the lion watched him. Now and then it let out a sound rather like a purr. After a while, the swelling in the paw seemed to go down a bit and it did not look quite so black as before. Androclus felt thankful, too, to see that there was less pain in the lion's eyes.

Finally, he made a pad out of one of the wet strips of cloth, placed it over the wound and then wrapped the paw in another strip.

"That will protect it until it heals," he told the lion. 'In a strange way,' Androclus thought, 'the lion seems to understand.'

The lion was obviously feeling a lot better. It got up on three legs and began to hobble around. It hobbled forward a few steps and before long, the lion was moving along the rocky path, away from where Androclus stood watching it. Then the lion began to move more quickly until it disappeared over a small hillock.

What Androclus did not know as he watched the lion was that three soldiers were watching *him*. They had spotted Androclus outside the cave and crept up unseen while he was tending the lion. Now the soldiers were hiding behind rocks further up the hill, waiting until the lion disappeared from sight.

"All right," one of the soldiers muttered to the others when the lion had gone. "Let's grab him!"

Androclus heard the soldiers as they scrambled from behind the rock, but by the time he started to run away, it was too late. One of the soldiers grabbed Androclus round the waist and threw him on to the rocky ground. The other two held him down, while the soldier tied his wrists together with rope.

Androclus felt like weeping. It was so unjust that his act of kindness towards the lion should end like this.

One of the soldiers gave Androclus a rough push.

"Your master, Publius Sirius, wants to see you," he told Androclus. "He's got a very special punishment for runaway slaves!"

"What is it? What's going to happen to me?" Androclus gasped, knowing how cruel Publius Sirius was.

The soldiers laughed. "You'll see!" they sneered. "And when you do, you'll be sorry you ever thought of running away."

Three weeks later, Androclus sat on the floor of a large underground cellar with his hands chained to a ring that was sunk into the stone wall. Nearby sat another man, chained in the same way, and next to him, another. From above their heads, they could all hear the crowd chattering and laughing in their seats around the amphitheatre. From the excitement in their voices it was clear that the crowd expected good, blood-thirsty sport. After all, it wasn't every day that runaway slaves and ferocious lions were put into the arena together. Emperor Tiberius himself was coming to watch.

This was certainly a special punishment, just as Publius Sirius had planned. 'This time,' Androclus thought grimly, 'there is no hope of escape.'

There was a sudden burst of cheering from above, in the amphitheatre.

"The Emperor's arrived," the man next to Androclus whispered. "It won't be long now!"

A few moments later, the bolts on the cellar door were drawn back and the door creaked open. A troop of soldiers marched in and started unchaining Androclus and the other slaves. They were pushed into the centre of the cellar and a large grille at the end was pulled up. Beyond it lay the sand-covered arena, the eagerly awaiting crowd of spectators – and the lions. Androclus

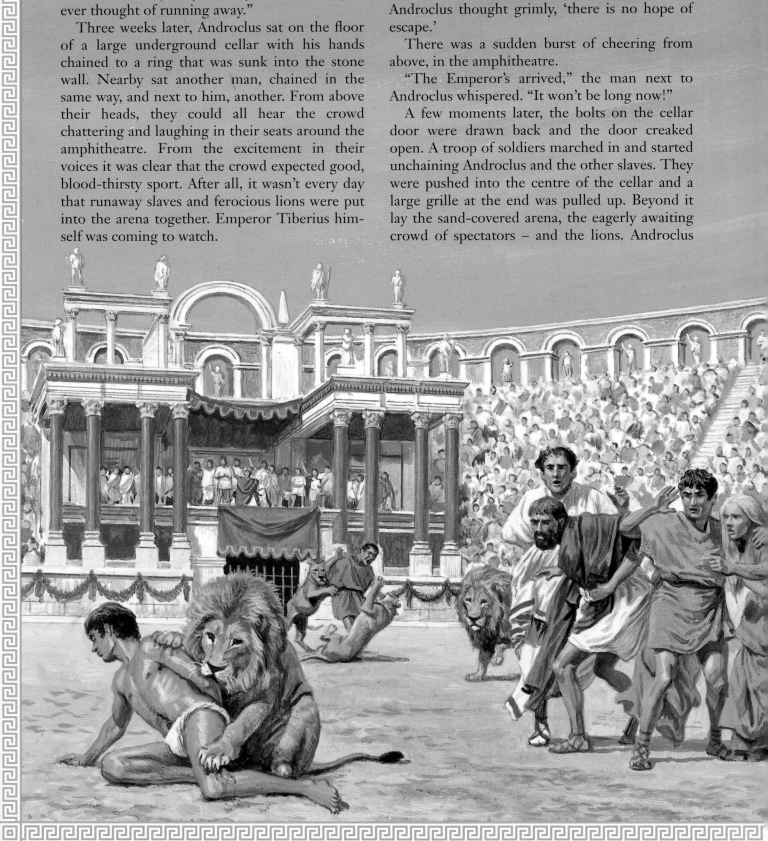

felt a sharp push in his back and he stumbled forward. With the other slaves, he emerged into the brilliant sunshine that filled the arena. As the crowd spotted them, they let out a great yell of excitement.

There was a scraping sound from across the arena and a grille at the opposite end moved up. At once, ten or twelve lions came bounding out and started racing across the sand to where the slaves stood, petrified with fear.

The first lion to reach them leapt upwards and Androclus got a quick glimpse of the underneath of its belly as it landed on a slave and knocked him to the ground. Androclus and the rest of the slaves started to run. They ran out into the centre or round the sides of the arena.

The crowd shouted and clapped as they watched. The laughed at those slaves who tried to climb the walls in an attempt to escape, only to have lions leap up at them and pull them back.

Suddenly, Androclus saw a lion leap towards him. He tried to get out of the way, but the great animal was upon him before he could do so. Androclus felt the hot pain as the lion's claws tore into his arm. Any moment now, and Androclus would feel the lion's sharp, curved fangs sinking into his flesh.

But nothing like that occurred. Instead, to Androclus' amazement, the lion started licking the scratches on his arm. The crowd saw what was happening, and their shouts of excitement turned to shouts of astonishment.

When the lion had finished licking Androclus' arm, it lay down next to him and put its paw across his chest, as if to protect him.

Even the Emperor Tiberius was on his feet, mouth wide open with amazement. Nothing like this had ever been seen in the amphitheatre before. Androclus put his hands up and turned the lion's face towards him.

"I know you," Androclus said. "And you haven't forgotten me."

The lion purred as Androclus lifted his paw and looked at it. There, sure enough, was a small, round hole in one of his pads. This was the lion Androclus had tended at the cave. Now it was showing how grateful it was. Not only had the lion not killed Androclus, but it was growling fiercely at the other lions.

The whole amphitheatre was in an uproar now. The Emperor ordered the animal keepers to drive the other lions back into their cellar. The slaves who were unharmed stood and wept with relief at their unexpected escape from death.

Androclus got to his feet, and dusted the sand off his tunic. The lion sat meekly beside him, looking up at him with adoring eyes. Everyone in the crowd was clapping. Even the Emperor joined in, and a tremendous cheering broke out as Androclus walked round the ring with the lion following him like a faithful dog.

Emperor Tiberius was so amused that he gave Androclus his freedom.

"A man who can tame the wildest of beasts cannot be a slave," the Emperor told the delighted Androclus.

Androclus was even more delighted when the Emperor let him keep the lion as his own. Afterwards, the two of them became well known in Rome. Wherever Androclus went, the lion went too. No one was afraid to meet them in the street, even when Androclus did not put the lion on a lead. After all, wasn't it the tamest lion ever seen in Rome?